The Best Ever Book of

FUNNY POEMS

*Also by Brian Moses and available from
Macmillan Children's Books*

Lost Magic: The Very Best of Brian Moses

The Best Ever Book of FUNNY POEMS

CHOSEN BY BRIAN MOSES

MACMILLAN CHILDREN'S BOOKS

First published 2021 by Macmillan Children's Books
an imprint of Pan Macmillan
The Smithson, 6 Briset Street, London EC1M 5NR
EU representative: Macmillan Publishers Ireland Limited,
Mallard Lodge, Lansdowne Village, Dublin 4
Associated companies throughout the world
www.panmacmillan.com

ISBN 978-1-5290-4971-8

1 3 5 7 9 8 6 4 2

A CIP catalogue record for this book is available from the British Library.

Printed and bound by CPI Group (UK) Ltd, Croydon CR0 4YY

Contents

The Red Ear Blows Its Nose: Silly & Even Sillier Poems

I Once Had a Snail for a Pet: Funny Poems About Pets

The Animal Kingdom's a Hoot:
Funny Poems About Creatures

The Headmaster's Welcome:
Funny Poems About School

My Dad's More Embarrassing Than Your Dad: Funny Poems About Families

Perfect Rhymes with Oranges Are Comparatively Rare: Funny Poems About Poems

And That ... Is What I Call a Happy Ending: Funny Poems About Fantasy & Fairy Tales

If You Dare to Dine with Dinosaurs: Funny Poems About Dinosaurs & Dragons

A Ghost Went Out Haunting One Saturday Night: Funny Spooky Poems

You Pulled Me Out of a Black Hole: Funny Poems About Space

The Red Ear Blows Its Nose:

Silly & Even Sillier Poems

Ladies and Jelly Spoons

Ladies and jelly spoons:
I come before you
To stand behind you
And tell you something
I know nothing about.

Next Thursday,
The day after Friday,
There'll be a mothers' meeting
For fathers only.

Wear your best clothes,
If you haven't any.
And if you can come,
Please stay at home.

Admission is free:
You can pay at the door
We'll give you a seat
So you can sit on the floor.

It makes no difference where you sit;
The man in the gallery is sure to spit.

Anon

Reasons Why Your Train Was Late This Morning

The train on platform one
had a note from its mum.

The train on platform two
went up in a puff of smoke,
someone said *you know who* was on board.
Don't say his name,
it may not be a joke.

The train on platform three
stopped for a cup of tea,
a sandwich, a cake and two bags of crisps,
then went for a dip in the sea.

The train that should have been on platform four
found a secret door to another dimension,
now it's millions of light years away.

The train on platforms five, six and seven
came in sideways.

You missed the train on platform eight,
it left already, you were late.

Brian Moses

Uffington

There's a place called Uffington
where the boys are scruffington,
the girls are tuffington,
the dogs are wuffington,
the cats are fluffington,
the schools are ruffington,
the teachers gruffington.
There's really nuffington
you can do but huffington
and puffington
and say that's enuffington
of all the stuffington
that goes on in Uffington.

Myles McLeod

Tarzan and Jane

Snakes in the grass go hiss-hiss-hiss
Tarzan and Jane go kiss-kiss-kiss.

Anon

What's Mine

Things that no one's said before
include, 'The red ear blows its nose',
'I noodled waffles to the door',
'The slipper broke my shoulder's toes',

'But what about the squiggly spoon
that ate a penguin's piece of pie
beneath a buttered slice of moon
beyond a sloppy slab of sky?'

Though almost everything's been said,
'How sad the pizza's climbed the peak
and cheese now tops the oyster bed'
are words I am the first to speak.

And surely if I say the fox
has cartwheeled through the slide trombone
in search of nylon bowling socks,
these words belong to me alone.

Robert Schechter

Hamster Man

He's one-half hamster, one-half man,
he rides around in a caravan.

He's six-foot tall with furry ears
(and 107 in hamster years).

He answers the phone with three short squeaks.
He stores ham sandwiches in his cheeks.

His wits are as sharp as his two front teeth
but he turns to mush when scratched beneath

his chin. Oh Hamster Man's the real deal,
running all night on his giant wheel.

He's one of a kind, there ain't no clan
of rodent men, just Hamster Man.

Kate Wakeling

8

The Jumblies

I

They went to sea in a Sieve, they did,
  In a Sieve they went to sea:
In spite of all their friends could say,
On a winter's morn, on a stormy day,
  In a Sieve they went to sea!
And when the Sieve turned round and round,
And every one cried, 'You'll all be drowned!'
They called aloud, 'Our Sieve ain't big,
But we don't care a button! we don't care a fig!
  In a Sieve we'll go to sea!'
   Far and few, far and few,
    Are the lands where the Jumblies live;
   Their heads are green, and their hands are blue,
    And they went to sea in a Sieve.

II

They sailed away in a Sieve, they did,
  In a Sieve they sailed so fast,
With only a beautiful pea-green veil
Tied with a riband by way of a sail,
  To a small tobacco-pipe mast;
And every one said, who saw them go,
'O won't they be soon upset, you know!

For the sky is dark, and the voyage is long,
And happen what may, it's extremely wrong
   In a Sieve to sail so fast!'
      Far and few, far and few,
         Are the lands where the Jumblies live;
      Their heads are green, and their hands are blue,
         And they went to sea in a Sieve.

III

The water it soon came in, it did,
   The water it soon came in;
So to keep them dry, they wrapped their feet
In a pinky paper all folded neat,
   And they fastened it down with a pin.
And they passed the night in a crockery-jar,
And each of them said, 'How wise we are!
Though the sky be dark, and the voyage be long,
Yet we never can think we were rash or wrong,
   While round in our Sieve we spin!'
      Far and few, far and few,
         Are the lands where the Jumblies live;
      Their heads are green, and their hands are blue,
         And they went to sea in a Sieve.

IV

And all night long they sailed away;
  And when the sun went down,
They whistled and warbled a moony song
To the echoing sound of a coppery gong,
  In the shade of the mountains brown.
'O Timballo! How happy we are,
When we live in a sieve and a crockery-jar,
And all night long in the moonlight pale,
We sail away with a pea-green sail,
  In the shade of the mountains brown!'
    Far and few, far and few,
      Are the lands where the Jumblies live;
    Their heads are green, and their hands are blue,
      And they went to sea in a Sieve.

V

They sailed to the Western Sea, they did,
  To a land all covered with trees,
And they bought an Owl, and a useful Cart,
And a pound of Rice, and a Cranberry Tart,
  And a hive of silvery Bees.
And they bought a Pig, and some green Jack-daws,
And a lovely Monkey with lollipop paws,
And forty bottles of Ring-Bo-Ree,
  And no end of Stilton Cheese.
    Far and few, far and few,

Are the lands where the Jumblies live;
Their heads are green, and their hands are blue,
And they went to sea in a Sieve.

VI

And in twenty years they all came back,
  In twenty years or more,
And every one said, 'How tall they've grown!'
For they've been to the Lakes, and the Torrible Zone,
  And the hills of the Chankly Bore;
And they drank their health, and gave them a feast
Of dumplings made of beautiful yeast;
And everyone said, 'If we only live,
We too will go to sea in a Sieve,—
  To the hills of the Chankly Bore!'
    Far and few, far and few,
      Are the lands where the Jumblies live;
    Their heads are green, and their hands are blue,
      And they went to sea in a Sieve.

Edward Lear

Jabberwocky

'Twas brillig, and the slithy toves
    Did gyre and gimble in the wabe:
All mimsy were the borogoves,
    And the mome raths outgrabe.

'Beware the Jabberwock, my son!
    The jaws that bite, the claws that catch!
Beware the Jubjub bird, and shun
    The frumious Bandersnatch!'

He took his vorpal sword in hand;
    Long time the manxome foe he sought—
So rested he by the Tumtum tree
    And stood awhile in thought.

And, as in uffish thought he stood,
    The Jabberwock, with eyes of flame,
Came whiffling through the tulgey wood,
    And burbled as it came!

One, two! One, two! And through and through
    The vorpal blade went snicker-snack!
He left it dead, and with its head
    He went galumphing back.

'And hast thou slain the Jabberwock?
    Come to my arms, my beamish boy!
O frabjous day! Callooh! Callay!'
    He chortled in his joy.

'Twas brillig, and the slithy toves
    Did gyre and gimble in the wabe:
All mimsy were the borogoves,
    And the mome raths outgrabe.

Lewis Carroll

The Loch Ness Monster's Song

Sssnnnwhuffffll?
Hnwhuffl hhnnwfl hnfl hfl?
Gdroblboblhobngbl gbl gl g g g g glbgl.
Drublhaflablhaflubhafgabhaflhafl fl fl –
gm grawwwww grf grawf awfgm graw gm.
Hovoplodok – doplodovok – plovodokot-doplodokosh?
Splgraw fok fok splgrafhatchgabrlgabrl fok splfok!
Zgra kra gka fok!
Grof grawff gahf?
Gombl mbl bl –
blm plm,
blm plm,
blm plm,
blp.

Edwin Morgan

Silly dream

I once fell asleep while wide awake
after eating a cake that wasn't baked
I had chewed some water and drank some bread
before tucking myself in underneath my bed

I had a sweet nightmare the monsters were scared
they screamed and begged that they'd be spared
I went sleepwalking to get some air
Came back home and got sat on by a chair

The TV watched me while chewing popcorn
The fire in the fireplace rubbed its hands to keep warm
The book on the table opened up, tried to read the room
the carpet whispered 'I've got it covered' but just laid
    there, blue

I got up from under the chair and landed on the roof
I looked up and the floor was above my head then 'poof'
it all went up in smoke, they say there's no fire without it
did this really happen? Believe me, I really doubt it

Karl Nova

Bengal

There once was a man of Bengal
Who was asked to a fancy dress ball;
    He murmured: 'I'll risk it
    And go as a biscuit . . .'
But a dog ate him up in the hall.

Anon

Roast Dinner

Said a guest to his cannibal host,
('twas a very regrettable boast):
'If you're stuck what to cook
From your recipe book . . .
My wife makes a jolly nice roast!'

Graham Denton

Poor Ollie

A steamroller flattened poor Ollie,
They shovelled him up from the floor,
And trundled him home on a trolley
And then slid him under the door.

Colin West

I Once Had a
Snail for a Pet:

Funny Poems
About Pets

Slimed

I once had a snail for a pet.
Did he ooze with affection? You bet!
He slobbered me silly
With slime, thick and chilly –
Kisses I'll never forget.

B. J. Lee

Important points to consider when choosing a name for your Guinea Pig

1. As a general rule please do avoid Dimples, Pimples, Puffball and Sir Squeaks-a-lot.
2. Let's be honest. Have you ever met a successful Diddums, Plopsy, Fluffyface or Dumpling?
   Didn't think so!
3. For the more rotund Guinea Pig, sensitive about his weight, Fat Chap, Chubbkins and (would you believe) Blobert are quite simply OUT OF THE QUESTION.
4. Would you like to introduce yourself (to your future wife) as Prince Pudding Pants III?
   No? Neither did he.
5. Finally, please be aware that no good will ever come from naming your new pet, Killer, Fang, Lucifer or . . . The Beast.
   You have been warned.

Yours sincerely,
(from one who knows)

Scarface McSquidgybot Stevenson

Julie Douglas

Pet Peeve

Keeping
a chameleon
for a pet

is something
that I now
regret.

At first,
as far as
I could tell,

he seemed
to blend in
very well,

but he's
changed a lot
in many ways

I've not
seen him now
for fourteen days.

Brian Bilston

The Invisible Man's Invisible Dog

My invisible dog is not much fun.
I don't know if he's sad or glum.
I don't know if, when I pat his head,
I'm really patting his bum instead.

Brian Patten

Kittens for Sale

I know you said I couldn't
and you said I shouldn't beg.
You said, to sharpen up their claws,
they use a sofa leg.
You said they shed in winter,
and you said they could have fleas.
You said that Dad's allergic,
and they make him sniff and sneeze.

So now you're sort of angry.
I can tell you want to shout.
But, Mom, I have some happy news,
so please just hear me out.
It's not a great catastrophe
or such an awful fix.
That cat had seven kittens,
and I only brought home six!

Eric Ode

27

My Flat Cat

I have a cat.
My cat is flat.
He sleeps beneath
the bathroom mat.

He slides around
upon the ground
without the slightest
striding sound.

He only eats
the flattest meats
and thin and wispy
kitty treats.

He once was fat
but now my cat
is totally,
completely flat.

He got so slim,
so flat and trim
the day my Great Dane
sat on him.

Kenn Nesbitt

There's a Hamster in the Fast Lane

(After seeing a newspaper report of a hamster in a hamster ball spotted rolling down the street.)

The speed cameras are flashing
But they can't identify
A hamster in the fast lane
As he roly-polys by.

He doesn't show a number
And shades obscure his eyes.
Police reports all tell of some
Boy racer in disguise.

For everyone who sees him
He's the cause of mirth and mayhem.
He's passing big fat four-wheel drives
By rolling underneath them.

No more tickles on the tummy,
No more crummy little cage.
One hundred miles an hour at least,
Fuelled by hamster rage.

He's passing open tops,
He's passing executive cars.
His energy is endless,
No sleep till Zanzibar!

He's belting down the bypass
Like a speed king on a track,
Unsure of where he's going
But he knows he won't be back!

Brian Moses

Miss King's Kong

It was our 'Bring your pet to school' day

Warren's wolfhound was chasing Paula's poodle
Paula's poodle was chasing Colin's cat
Colin's cat was chasing Harriet's hamster
And Harriet's hamster was chasing Benny's beetle

Suzie's snake was trying to swallow
Freddie's frog, Percy's parrot, Rebecca's rabbit
Belinda's bat, Gordon's goat, Peter's pig
And part of Patricia's pony

When all of a sudden everything stopped

Miss King had brought her pet to school as well
Miss King's Kong stood there
Roared and beat his chest

Miss King smiled
Miss King's Kong smiled too
As he swung from the light, eating bananas

Everything was quiet
Until the headmaster came in with his pet
Mr Lock's Ness . . . was a real monster

Paul Cookson

Our Hippopotamus

We thought a lively pet to keep
Might be a hippopotamus,
Now see him sitting in a heap,
And notice at the bottom – us.

Colin West

Dog's Swear Words

Furballs
Catsbum
It's-too-wet
Catswee
Ratspoo
Bath-time
Vet

Roger Stevens

The Animal Kingdom's a Hoot:

Funny Poems About Creatures

Emus

To amuse
      emus
on warm summer nights

      Kiwis
do wiwis
from spectacular heights.

Roger McGough

The Hippopotamus's Warning

A jungle panorama
Looking calm, no hint of drama,
But deep down in the river, just beware,
There's a herd of hippopotamus,
There might be quite a lot of us,
And pretty soon we're coming up for air.

Val Neubecker

Poem to answer the question: how old are fleas?

Adam
Had 'em.

Anon

Who's who?

Jemima Pugh never knew
a crocodile from an alligator.
So poor Miss Pugh didn't have a clue
which wriggled up the bank and ate her.

Alison Chisholm

The Animal Kingdom's a Hoot

The animal kingdom's a hoot
From the llama right up to the coot
Though earwigs and ants
Are totally pants
The hammerhead shark is a beaut.

Anon

Nobody Loves Me

Nobody loves me,
Everybody hates me,
I think I'll go and eat worms.

Big fat squishy ones,
Little thin skinny ones,
See how they wiggle and squirm.

Bite their heads off.
'Schlurp!' they're lovely,
Throw the tails away.

Nobody knows
How big I grows
On worms three times a day.

Anon

Eletelephony

Once there was an elephant,
Who tried to use the telephant –
No! No! I mean an elephone
Who tried to use the telephone –
(Dear me! I am not quite certain
That even now I've got it right.)

Howe'er it was, he got his trunk
Entangled in the telephunk;
The more he tried to get it free,
The louder buzzed the telephee –
(I fear I'd better drop the song
Of elepop and telephong!)

Laura E. Richards

lemmings

The tundra is a lemming's home,
He tunnels through the snow.
His thick fur helps to keep him warm
As he moves about below.

My mum says she likes lemmings,
Especially when squeezed . . .

No, No, No, dear, that's lemons!

What?

Lemons! L-E-M-O-N-S

Oh!
. . . I'm awful glad to hear that
And the lemmings will be pleased!

Doda Smith

A Goat in a landfill

A goat was in a landfill
eating garbage and debris
and came across a movie;
a discarded DVD.

He chewed the case and cover
and the flavour made him smile.
He took the disc between his lips
and nibbled for a while.

He thought, 'This film is brilliant;
full of action and suspense.
The story is exciting
and the fight scenes are intense.

'It's got a lot of comedy,
a touch of sweet romance,
and music so inspiring
it makes me want to dance.'

He gnawed a little longer
through some drama and a chase,
and finished off the movie
with a grin upon his face.

He gulped the closing credits –
one more bite was all it took –
and thought, 'That film was awesome
but I still preferred the book.'

Kenn Nesbitt

A Quick Thought About Birds

The sky's so great.
The cloud's so low.
The winter's here.
The smart birds go

south to seek
the fleeing sun.
The ones that stay
behind are dumb.

A. F. Harrold

Haik-Haik-Haik

Mallards laughing in
The reeds: A duckling must have
Quacked a little joke.

Norman Silver

The Firefly

The firefly is a funny bug,
He hasn't any mind;
He blunders all the way through life
With his headlight on behind.

Anon

Recipe for a Wasp

Take a gallon of petrol
from the BMW
that overtook your dad on the motorway
that time he said a rude word.
Your baby brother's tantrum
the morning your mum went back to work,
an argument with your best friend,
and your sister's smirk.
Boil violently.
Sieve the mixture through the jumper your gran made.
The itchy one with yellow and black stripes
and a head-hole that's too tight.
Stir in some English mustard with a freshly sharpened
  pencil.
This *must* be HB.

Next you will need:
The tick of the clock outside the head teacher's office
Some nails bitten to the quick
The smell of hospitals
Lego trodden on in bare feet
and a Sunday evening sense of doom.
Beat with a splintery wooden spoon.
Pour into your mould
and bake at ten thousand degrees Fahrenheit
in the centre of the sun.
Allow to cool a little, and admire your insect.
A heat-seeking missile
in a bombshell body.

Release at a picnic . . .

and **RUN.**

Sarah Ziman

Snowing Polar Bears

It's raining cats and dogs
and it's snowing polar bears.
Wombats are whirling in the wind
and it's hailing hairy hares.

Tigers are twisting through tornadoes,
elephants are crashing through thunder.
Leopards are leaping through lightning bolts.
The skies are full of wonder.

Camels, crows and chameleons
are camouflaged in the fog,
squirrels stretched out in the sunshine
and hedgehogs enjoying a jog.

Cuckoos are canoodling in cumulus clouds
and snakes are swept up in a storm.
Meerkats are mingling under moonlit skies –
together they keep each other warm.

There are hummingbirds hovering in a heatwave
trying their best to cool down,
and a tsunami of sardines are swirling their way
through the rivers that run through the town,

So I think I might stay in today,
Close the curtains, switch on the TV.
Not that I'm scared to go out, of course,
It's just a bit too wild for me.

Peter Cole

A Vain Polar Bear

A vain polar bear, name of Lily,
Liked clothes that were flimsy and frilly,
She swapped her thick fleece
For a lacy two-piece,
So she's chic but exceedingly chilly.

Julia Rawlinson

The Hyena

The hyena has neither charm nor wit,
Beauty and courage? He hasn't a bit,
In the animal world he has no clout,
So I don't know what he's laughing about.

Valerie Bloom

Elephant Cleaners

The elephants empty the bins in twos
then wash the floors and clean the loos
they wipe the tops with hairy mops
one works hard whilst the other stops
and yet the truth I must confess
is that they leave the house a mess.

Dom Conlon

I Stood on the Ceiling

I stood on the ceiling for seventeen minutes.
I walked up a lavender wall.
I danced on a doughnut with strawberry filling
and touched every light in the hall.
I sat on a mushroom and anchovy pizza.
I spun and dove into a pie.
I love being me! Yes, I'm happy and free!
It's incredible being a fly!

Darren Sardelli

The Headmaster's Welcome:

Funny Poems About School

The Headmaster's Welcome

Parents and fool governors
we spank you all for humming.
We hope you like our concert
when the steel band will be plumbing,
the choir will be flinging us
a booty full holed song
and everyone's ignited
to join in and sling a pong!

Jill Townsend

Where Teachers Keep Their Pets

Mrs Cox has a fox
nesting in her curly locks.

Mr Spratt's tabby cat
sleeps beneath his bobble hat.

Mrs Cahoots has various newts
swimming in her zip-up boots.

Mr Spry has Fred his fly
eating food stains from his tie.

Mrs Groat shows off her stoat
round the collar of her coat.

Mr Spare's got grizzly bears
hiding in his spacious flares.

And . . .

Mrs Vickers has a stick insect called 'Stickers'
And she keeps it in her . . .

Paul Cookson

Cakes in the Staffroom

Nothing gets teachers more excited
than cakes in the staffroom at break time.
Nothing gets them more delighted
than the sight of plates
piled high with jammy doughnuts
or chocolate cake

It's an absolute stampede
as the word gets round quickly,

And it's 'Oooh these are really delicious,'
and, 'Aaah these doughnuts are great.'

And you hear them say, 'I really shouldn't'
or 'Just a tiny bit, I'm on a diet.'

Really, it's the only time they're quiet
when they're cramming cakes into their mouths,
when they're wearing a creamy moustache
or the jam squirts out like blood,
or they're licking chocolate
from their fingers.

You can tell when they've been scoffing,
they get lazy in literacy,
sleepy in silent reading,
nonsensical in numeracy,
look guilty in assembly.

But nothing gets teachers more excited
than cakes in the staffroom at break time,
unless of course,
it's wine in the staffroom at lunchtime!

Brian Moses

Instructions for the First Day at Monster School

1. Don't sit on a classmate
2. Keep your tail to yourself
3. Howling in assembly is forbidden
4. Sticking pencils/classroom equipment/teachers up your nose is not funny
5. Nor is sticking lumps of ear wax on the teacher's chair
6. No eating in the classroom – anyone caught eating someone else's homework/book bag/ear will be sent to the Headmonster
7. The lollipop lady's STOP sign is not edible
8. Don't drink the water from the toilet
9. All fire breathers MUST sit at the front of the classroom
10. Don't eat your teacher . . . or anyone else's

Kate Snow

Make Sure You Get to Class on Time

Our teacher is a cannibal.
She eats us if we're late.
At the start of the year there were 30 of us.
Now there's only eight.

Peter Cole

Science Lesson

We've done 'Water' and 'Metals' and 'Plastic'.
Today, it is the turn of 'Elastic':
Sir sets up a test . . .
Wow, that was the best –
he whizzed through the window. Fantastic!

Mike Johnson

Callum's Homework

Dear Miss Price,
This story sounds unbelievable
But every word is true
My poor Callum just finished his homework
When out of the window it flew!

Over the wall to Miss Buttons
Across her award-winning veg
On top of her dustbins and under her car
Got stuck in her hawthorn hedge!

As Callum reached out to grab it
Whoosh! The paper again took flight
Callum gave chase for miles and miles
His homework was now a kite!

Then, my Callum spotted his homework
On top of the village church spire
There gathered an anxious crowd below
As my Callum climbed higher and higher!

Poor Callum had to admit defeat
As the homework took off again
Over the sea to the Isle of Wight
To Ireland or France or Spain!

There is only one word for my Callum, Miss Price
A HERO, through and through
The story of my Callum's homework
Unbelievable, but true.

Debra Bertulis

Making a Meal of It

What did you do at school today?

Played football.

Where are you going now?

To play football.

What time will you be back?

After football.

Football! Football! Football!

That's all I ever hear.

Well?

Well don't be late for tea.

OK

We're having football casserole.

Eh?

Followed by football crumble.

What?

Washed down with . . .

As if I can't guess!

Nice pot of . . .

I'm not listening!

. . . tea.

Bernard Young

The School Goalie's Reasons ...
why each goal shouldn't have been a goal in the match that ended 14-0 to the visiting team

1   It wasn't fair. I wasn't ready ...
2   Their striker was offside. It was obvious ...
3   Phil got in my way, he always gets in my way, he should be dropped ...
4   had something in my eye ...
5   I hadn't recovered from the last one that went in, or the one before that ...
6   thought I heard our head teacher calling my name ...
7   Somebody exploded a blown-up crisp bag behind me ...
8   There was a beetle on the pitch, I didn't want to tread on it ...
9   Somebody exploded another blown-up crisp bag behind me ...
10 That girl in Year 5 was smiling at me. I don't like her doing that ...
11 The goalposts must have been shifted, they weren't as wide as that before ...
12 thought I saw a UFO fly over the school.
13 There was a dead ringer for Harry Kane watching us, he was spooky ...

And goal number 14?
  It just wasn't a goal, I'm sorry, it just wasn't a goal
  and that's that . . .
  O.K.?

Brian Moses

Tables

Headmaster a come, mek has'e! Sit down!
Jo, mind yuh bruck Jane collar bone.
Tom, tek yuh foot off o' de desk,
Sandra Wallace, mi know yuh vex
But beg yuh get off o' Joseph head.
Tek de lizard off o' Sue neck, Ted!
Sue, mi dear, don' bawl so loud,
Thomas, why yuh put de toad
Eena Elvira sandwich bag?
Jim, what yuh gwine do wid dat bull-frog?
Tek it off mi chair, yuh mad?
Yuh chair small, May, but it not dat bad
Dat yuh haffe siddung pon de floor!
Jim, don' squeeze de frog unda de door
Put it through de window – no, no, Les!
Mi know yuh hungry, but Mary yeas
Won' fill yuh up, so spit it out.
Now go wash de blood out o' yuh mout'.
Hortense, tek Mary to de nurse.
Nick, tek yuh han' outa Mary purse
Ah wonder who tell all o' yuh
Sey dat dis classroom is a zoo?
Quick! Headmaster comin' through de door.
'Two ones are two, two twos are four.'

Valerie Bloom

73

School Photo Day

Here's a tale of Meryl Rose
Who liked to push things up her nose . . .
    Lego, biscuits
        Beads and bread –
            Rattled round inside her head.

A foolish girl – who wasted days
Playing with her silly craze –

    Until upon school photo day
    She got the hamster out to play,
    And with a grin and Meryl pout
    She pushed poor Hammy up her snout!

'Look this way,' called photo man
'Smile or giggle if you can . . .'

Sweet Meryl posed
    With smile
        And pout –

And half a hamster hanging out!

Peter Dixon

Thirteen Questions You Should Be Prepared to Answer If You Lose Your Ears at School

Are they clearly named?
When did you notice they were missing?
Were they fixed on properly?
What colour are they?
What size?
Have you looked in the playground?
Did you take them off for P.E.?
Could somebody else have picked them up by mistake?
Have you felt behind the radiators?
Did you lend them to anybody?
Have you searched the bottom of your bag?
Does the person you sit next to have a similar pair?
Are you sure you brought them to school with you this
    morning?

John Coldwell

Erasing the Board

I thought my teacher would be proud
when I erased the board.
I thought she'd say, 'Terrific Job!'
and give me a reward.
I thought the students in my class
would smile, clap, and cheer.
I never thought the chalkboard
would completely disappear.

Darren Sardelli

My Dad's More Embarrassing Than Your Dad:

Funny Poems About Families

Mum Used Pritt Stick

Mum used Pritt Stick
Instead of lipstick
Then went and kissed my dad

Two days passed
Both stuck fast
The longest snog they ever had

Paul Cookson

The Car Trip

Mum says:
'Right, you two,
this is a very long car journey.
I want you two to be good.
I'm driving and I can't drive properly
if you two are going mad in the back.
Do you understand?'

So we say,
'OK, Mum, OK. Don't worry,'
and off we go.

And we start The Moaning:
Can I have a drink?
I want some crisps.
Can I open my window?
He's got my book.
Get off me.
Ow, that's my ear!

And Mum tries to be exciting:
'Look out the window
there's a lamp-post.'

And we go on with The Moaning:
Can I have a sweet?
He's sitting on me.

Are we nearly there?
Don't scratch.
You never tell him off.
Now he's biting his nails.
I want a drink. I want a drink.

And Mum tries to be exciting again:
'Look out the window.
There's a tree.'

And we go on:
My hands are sticky.
He's playing with the door handle now.
I feel sick.
Your nose is all runny.
Don't pull my hair.

He's touching me, Mum.
That's really dangerous, you know.
Mum, he's spitting.

And Mum says:
'Right, I'm stopping the car.
I AM STOPPING THE CAR.'

She stops the car.

'Now, if you two don't stop it
I'm going to put you out of the car
and leave you by the side of the road.'

He started it.
I didn't. He started it.

'I don't care who started it
I can't drive properly
if you two go mad in the back.
Do you understand?'

And we say:
OK, Mum, OK. Don't worry.

Can I have a drink?

Michael Rosen

Crossing the line

An imaginary line runs down the back seat of our car.
Our mother warned, 'Don't cross that line!' It's kept
the peace . . . so far.

Eons have elapsed, and I've not budged a single
inch,

but my elbow burns to give a jab; my fingers itch to
pinch.

My sister's sticking out her tongue; I really want to
kick her.

One quick flick across this line might stop her
little snicker.

I'm caving under pressure; boy, this trip seems
much too slow.

I've made it to the corner . . . just five hundred miles
to go!

Michelle Schaub

My Mum's Put Me on the Transfer List

On offer:
One nippy striker, ten years old
has scored seven goals this season
has nifty footwork and a big smile
knows how to dive in the penalty box
can get filthy and muddy in two minutes
guaranteed to wreck his kit each week
this is a FREE TRANSFER
but he comes with running expenses
weeks of washing shirts and shorts
socks and vests, a pair of trainers
needs to scoff huge amounts
of chips and burgers, beans and apples
pop and cola, crisps and oranges
endless packets of chewing gum.
This offer open until the end of the season
I'll have him back then
at least until the cricket starts.
Any takers?

David Harmer

When My Little Sister Sings

When my little sister sings
I'd like to think of lovely things
Morning birdsong, angel wings
A nightingale, a bell that rings
Music fit for queens and kings
When my little sister sings

But these are not the sounds she brings
More like boingy rusty springs
The noises caused by nettle stings
Or cats that scratch on violins
Then scrape their claws on broken strings
Creaking chains on squeaking swings

I'd rather hear *anything*
Than listen to my sister sing

Paul Cookson

My Brother's Not Evolved Yet

My brother's not evolved yet.
He lies in bed all day.
He has an old and musty smell
that will not go away.

He shuffles down the hall
and beats his chest just like an ape.
He will not get a haircut
so his head's a monkey shape.

He grunts in monosyllables.
He cannot say 'hello'.
He won't say 'please' or 'thank you' –
these are words he doesn't know.

He drags his knuckles on the floor.
His chin's encased in fluff.
He pillages the fridge to binge
until he's had enough.

I'm so fed up of living with
this simian buffoon.
My brother's not evolved yet.
I hope it happens soon.

Joshua Seigal

My Dad's More Embarrassing Than Your Dad

My Dad's more embarrassing than your Dad.
Does yours get all your friends' names really wrong?

My Dad has to be more embarrassing than your Dad.
Does yours try to sing your favourite song?

My Dad is way more embarrassing than your Dad.
Does yours wear sandals with socks on the sands?

My Dad is so much more embarrassing than your Dad.
Does yours dance with just his feet and his hands?

My Dad is definitely more embarrassing than your Dad.
Does yours always ask you how to use the computer?

My Dad is a trillion times more embarrassing than your
*   Dad.*
Does yours try to wiggle his hooter?

Chrissie Gittins

Dad, Don't Dance

Whatever you do, don't dance, Dad
Whatever you do, don't dance.
Don't wave your arms
Like a crazy buffoon
Displaying your charms
By the light of the moon
Trying to romance
a lady baboon
Whatever you do, don't dance.

When you try to dance
Your left leg retreats
And your right leg starts to advance
Whatever you do, don't dance, Dad
Has a ferret crawled into your pants?
Or maybe a hill full of ants
Don't samba
Don't rumba
You'll tumble
And stumble
Whatever you do, Dad, don't dance

Don't glide up the aisle with a trolley
Or twirl the girl on the till
You've been banned from dancing in Tesco
'Cos your tango made everyone ill.

Whatever you do, don't dance, Dad
Whatever you do, don't dance
Don't make that weird face
Like you ate a sour plum
Don't waggle your hips
And stick out your bum
But most of all – PLEASE –
Don't smooch with Mum!
Whatever the circumstance.
Whatever you do –
Dad, don't dance.

Roger Stevens

Zach's Diary

Dear Diary, it's been quite a year
Some funny things have happened here
It started when I noticed that
My mum was getting very fat

The months went by and it got worse
Until it looked like Mum might burst
I think her tummy really shocked her
So my Daddy called the doctor

Granny came and off they went
But I know how their time was spent
To make my Mummy small and thin
The doctor popped her with a pin

And just like any burst balloon
She went off whizzing round the room.
It worked! And next time I saw Mummy
She had lost her giant tummy

But then the docs (or nurses maybe)
Brought my mum a tiny baby
'Zach,' she said, 'here's baby Lili.'
I thought she looked pink and silly

Now Mum's home. I'm glad, I missed her
And she's brought this baby sister
I never knew, I'm ashamed to say
That hospitals did takeaway

Mary Evans

Sold!

I sold my bike, I sold my bed,
I sold my soggy phone.
I sold the telly, sold the bread,
and sold a battle drone.
I sold the fridge and teddy bears,
I sold an oven mitt.
I sold the couch, I sold the chairs –
there's nowhere left to sit.

I sold a Chelsea football, signed,
I sold a hiking pack.
I sold the baby, changed my mind,
and bought Elijah back.
I sold the sinks and garden gnomes,
I sold a pirate's gem.
I tried to sell my funny poems,
but no one wanted them.

I sold a bench and barbeque,
I sold a furry squid.
I sold my sister's secrets, too,
but only got a quid.
I sold Mom's shoes and lemon tree,
and sold my Dad's guitar.
They're really both upset with me –
I'd also sold their car.

I told them all the money went
to serve a worthy cause.
They hopped and screamed, 'It's all been spent?'
There was an awkward pause . . .
'To save endangered what?' they fumed,
'The giant humpback mouse?'
They tried to send me to my room . . .
but I had sold the house.

William Peery

Upgrading Granny

Granny's been to the hospital
She needed an upgrade again
Her body's been stripped and refitted
By an army of white-coated men

Her new teeth are pure carbon fibre
Her specs were designed with a laser
She can now bite through plates if she wants to
And her eyesight's as sharp as a razor

She's got digital hearing-aid power
And her pacemaker's nuclear I'm told
They replaced her hip with a stainless-steel joint
And her Zimmer's now radio-controlled

There was a special offer on memory
She got 64 gigs of it free
She can now recall where she left granddad
And that I owe her 35p

Her toilet's controlled by computer
Her electric shopping cart's fun
Her stairlift's got internet access
I can't wait till I'm ninety-one

Andy Seed

Grandpa's stories

Grandpa says he's so old
that when he was seven
he lived next door to Queen Victoria
they took the dinosaurs
for a walk in the park every morning
being quite small
Her Majesty had a lot of trouble
with the Tyrannosaurus Rex.

Grandpa says yesterday
a pirate ship sailed on the lake in the park,
a skull and crossbones flew from the mast
all the bloodthirsty crew
swarmed up the rigging, jumped
with pistols and cutlasses
into the playground, swung on the swings,
dug up the football pitch for treasure
marooned the first mate
on the traffic island across the road.

Grandpa says he knows for certain
a spaceship the size of a wheelie bin
landed on our school field last Thursday
slimy aliens slid like giant slugs
through a crack in the wall.
They searched the whole building for us kids
wanting to suck out our brains.
'But I'm not sure if you lot
have got any brains.' laughed Grandpa,

I really like listening to my Grandpa,
and all his stories are true.

David Harmer

Ten Torn Messages

Found on Shelf
(bottom half)

Delivery man is under the doormat

walking Dinner is in the oven

Bill is behind the clock

dustbin – expecting Granny soon!

fridge – needs warming!

the windows love Fred

sausages Please fetch washing in

the dentist can't stop

the dotted line Will see you at 5pm

forget to close the gate

Found in Bin
(top half)

Money for

Dog needs

Electricity

Please put rubbish in

Baby's bottle in

Please close

Have bought some

Am on my way to

Please sign on

Dog gone missing – you always

Celia Warren

Puzzle

I thought I was the biggest child
In our little family,
But Mum says Dad's the biggest child
So where does that leave me?

Brian Moses

Perfect Rhymes with Oranges Are Comparatively Rare:

Funny Poems About Poems

Perfect Rhymes
with Oranges Are
Comparatively Rare:

Funny Poems
About Poems

Common Problems Encountered in Writing Poetry

Problem 1: Writing Poems on the Walk to School

Writing poems on the walk to school
is not an easy thing to do at all.
The thing you need to mind the most
is bumping into a lam

Problem 2: Writing Poems on a Windy Day

The problem of writing poe ^{m} ^{s}

on a windy d ^{a} ^{y}

is that the stupid l e tte ^{r} ^{s}

start to b ^{lo} ^{w} ^{a} ^{w} ^{a} ^{y} .

Problem 3: Writing Poems in Hot Weather

The problem
of writingpoems
inhot weather
isthatthe words
getsweaty
and sticktogether.

Problem 4: Writing Poems in the Shape of Deciduous Trees

the pr blem of wr ting
po ms in the sha e of dec duous
trees is th t once there ar ives the
first stirri gs of the new a tumn breeze,
the p ems shake t emselves ge tly
unt l the letters loos n
like leaves,
and
they
start
to
fall
down
andthenmakeabigsoggymessontheground

Problem 5: Writing Poems in Invisible Ink

Brian Bilston

Poetry Postman

When the Poetry Postman
Had a hole in his bag
He kept losing letters
It was a bit of a rag

They ell to the groun
Through the ole in is ack
To pic hem al up
He ad t g bac

Som caught in he win
And ble up n he ir
Lik a warm of whit ees
They fle verywhere

He retrieved all the letters
Eventually
So he popped them in a postbox
And went home to tea

Roger Stevens

I Don't like Poetry

I don't like similes.
Every time I try to think of one
my brain feels like a vast, empty desert;
my eyes feel like raisins floating in an ocean;
my fingers feel like sweaty sausages.

I don't like metaphors.
Whenever I attempt them
a hammer starts beating in my chest;
lava starts running through my veins;
zombies have a fight in my stomach.

I don't like alliteration.
We learnt about it in school
but it's seriously, stupendously silly;
definitely drastically difficult;
terribly, troublingly tricky.

I don't like onomatopoeia.
I wish I could blow it up
with a ZAP! and a BANG! and a CRASH!;
a BOOM! and a CLANG! and a POW!;
a CLASH! and a BAM! and a THUD!

And I don't like repetition
I don't like repetition
I don't like repetition . . .

Joshua Seigal

Pantomime Poem*

I'm going to write a pantomime poem
OH NO YOU'RE NOT!
Oh yes I am!
One that will get everyone going
OH NO YOU'RE NOT!
Oh yes I am!

They'll be huge custard pies
And girls who slap thighs,
Men dressed in frocks
And bloomers with dots,
They'll be beanstalks and castles,
Some heroes, some rascals.
They'll be goodies to sing to
And villains BEHIND YOU!
They'll be eggs that are golden,
An actor who's an olden!
Cows all called Daisy
And songs that are crazy!

I'm going to write a pantomime poem
OH NO YOU'RE NOT!
Oh yes I am!
One that will get everyone going
OH NO YOU'RE NOT!
Oh yes I am!
OH NO YOU'RE NOT!
Oh yes I am!
OH NO YOU'RE NOT!
I just did!!

Coral Rumble

*Let your friends be your audience!

The Worst Poem Ever

Welcome to the worst poem that you've ever read
It should have been a masterpiece but I wrote this instead
The speling's truely awful
The simple rhythm's dull
The grammar's bad and it don't use no imagery at all

My friends who say it's brilliant are just being polite
My critics say it's dreadful and I'll admit they're right
It hasn't any subject
It hasn't any theme
And some of the lines don't rhyme either

I urge you to ignore it, it's nowhere near my best
The next poem I'm producing will make you more
    impressed
With what word can I end it?
I haven't got a clue
So I'm putting my pen down to leave that task to . . .

Neal Zetter

It's 'bring your brain to the library' day

It's *'bring your brain to the library'* day.
You can carry it there in your head,
Or a bus, or a car or a marmalade jar,
Or between two thick slices of bread.

You don't need to bring any stuff, anything –
Don't bring fingernails, bogies or hair.
But please bring your brain, we shan't tell you again,
For we don't have a brain going spare.

It's *'bring your brain to the library'* day.
For you need it to write out some rhymes.
Your kidney or spleen aren't required to be seen
As I've said to you several times.

Make sure that you've washed any gunky stuff off
For we don't want it dripping on books
And writing a rhyme when you're covered in slime
Is much harder to do than it looks.

It's *'bring your brain to the library'* day
To have some poetic tuition.
For even more fun, bring the brain of your mum
Or your dad, but please ask their permission.

With a brain you've enough to write poems and stuff.
Don't bring freckles or spots on your bum.
And have a good time with your brain writing rhymes
But please take it back home when you're done.

Mike Lucas

Why this poem ended up not being about oranges after all

Perfect rhymes with oranges
are comparatively rare.

I'd like to write about their zest,
instead I'm in despair;

about those pips, that yummy juice
I really couldn't care.

Their pith and flesh just leave me cold
I'm only too aware

to rhyme an orange with anything
I'll be tearing out my hair,

so I bought a rhyming dictionary
though I had no cash to spare

and looked up rhymes for oranges
but there were none in there

so in the end I just gave up.
This poem's about a pear.

Carole Bromley

115

And That . . .
Is What I Call a
Happy Ending:

Funny Poems About
Fantasy & Fairy Tales

The Storyland Sprint

*(To be read at great speed by your excited
Sports Reporter.)*

'And . . .
They're all lining up for the Grand Final –
Puss is adjusting his new, spiky boots,
(Plain green leather – no ankle-wings allowed).
Goldilocks is still puffing
After a training run with the Three Bears;
Snow White is giving her seven small friends
Some last-minute tips,
But Grumpy still doesn't look Happy.
Meanwhile, the Bad Fairy is being searched for
Go-Faster Spells;
The Little Pigs have been placed next to the Big Bad Wolf,
(Which CAN'T be right),
And Cinderella, wearing only one glass shoe,
Doesn't have a hope.

The last few runners are arriving, just in time!
Rapunzel's at the top of her stony tower,
She's blowing her whistle
And they're OFF . . .

Humpty Dumpty has fallen at the first fence;
The Ogre has tripped over a rusty old lamp,
And the Billy Goats are eating the Rickety-Rackety
Bridge!
But the Handsome Prince has hacked his way through
the thorn bushes,
He's tipped Sleeping Beauty out of her bed
And he's only just behind Tom Thumb,
Who is riding the world's fastest Rat!
It's neck and neck,
Only the Unicorn can overtake them now . . .

They've reached the last obstacle
(A rather tempting house made entirely of sweets).
The Rat can't resist,
The Unicorn is spiking peppermints,
The Prince is speeding ahead . . .
But wait
Who is this
Charging past the Troll and the
Ugly Sisters?

Running, in fact, as fast as he can –
Is it? Can it be?
YES!
It's the Gingerbread Man
Winning Rumpelstiltskin's sack of magic gold . . .
And that, my friends, is what I call
A Happy Ending.'

Clare Bevan

Epitaph for Humpty Dumpty

Beneath this wall there lies the shell
Of someone who had talents.
But (as you can probably tell)
One of them wasn't balance.

Rachel Rooney

Hickory, Dickory, Dock

Hickory, dickory, dock,
Two mice ran up the clock.
The clock struck one,
And the other one got away.

Anon

Coded Nursery Rhymes

Note: the code increases in difficulty, but here's a clue.
It's a bit fishy. See if you can crack it. Good luck!

1. An Easy One
Jack and Jill went up the fish
to fetch a pail of water.
Jack fell down and broke his fish
and Fish came tumbling after.

2. A Harder One
Little Fish Horner
sat fish a fish
eating a Christmas fish.
He fish in his fish
and fish fish fish plum
and said
'Fish fish fish fish fish I.'

3. A Very Hard One
Fish Fish
fish fish fish wall.
Fish Fish
fish fish great fish.
Fish fish fish fish
And fish fish fish fish
fish fish fish Fish fish again.

Ian McMillan

The Frog Prince

At first he cursed the witch's potion
which changed him from prince to frog.
He'd miss the cup final and skiing holiday
with his best old school mates.
He hated murky water and slime,
until he started to wallow in it.

He learnt to parachute out of trees
and leap over ducks and swans.
He didn't miss the gossipy glares
and beady stares, watching who he'd
danced with at a birthday party
or played tennis and croquet against.

He turned even greener at the memory of
oily handshakes and creepy politicians
and stuck-up daughters of wannabe in-laws.
He could go back to that hoity-toity life.

But for now he was happy
in his three-chambered heart
keeping a bulging eye on dragonflies,
singing into drainpipes, ribbiting at stars,
and hopping sideways to escape
the princesses' kisses.

David Keyworth

Three Bears vs Goldilocks

I did go into someone's house and, yes, I ate their
   porridge,
but only one small mouthful – it was lumpy, cold and
   horrid.

I did sit on their broken chair and watch a bit of telly,
but there was nothing good on and their living
   room was smelly.

I did decide to have a nap – I really was exhausted.
But then I made the bed and left. The story's been
   distorted.

I paid for bed and breakfast, so it's me who should be
   grouchy –
the food was gross, the service poor, the beds were old
   and slouchy.

The Three Bears need to drop their charges, or they'll be
   contested.
Their lodgings are so terrible, that THEY should be
   arrested.

Laura Mucha

Why the Hulk's Blue

'Being the Hulk is a test,'
Our green superhero confessed,
'And you'd be blue too
If each day you burst through
Your underpants, trousers and vest.'

Philip Waddell

Poem Written After Upsetting a Witch at the Watering Hole

I go to school every day.
I am not huge and great and grey.

My teeth are short and don't poke out
Of my mouth when I pout.

My ears are there at the side
But will not flap in shame or pride.

On my head, at the front,
Is a nose and not a trunk.

I've a hunch, I'm fairly sure,
I'm not an elephant anymore.

A. F. Harrold

When Midas Met Medusa

King Midas met Medusa
on a getaway vacation.
They liked each other instantly,
a true infatuation.
They gazed into each other's eyes
and kissed, but should have known.
Medusa turned to solid gold.
King Midas turned to stone.

Neal Levin

Twenty Ways to Avoid Monsters and Mythical Beasts

1. If your granny has a long thin furry face, consider the following: a) she's a werewolf. b) she's the big bad wolf. Either way, see a woodcutter before visiting her and under no circumstances comment on the size of her teeth.
2. Don't climb anything that grew taller than a house in one night.
3. Don't make bargains that include your first born child.
4. Don't eat buildings made of gingerbread.
5. Don't talk to witches; but take care to ignore them politely.
6. Don't play in caves unless you paid to get in.
7. If you do, avoid large eggs that smell of pumice.
8. If you find a trolls' nest don't dig up their gold.
9. Don't stand and howl at the moon.
10. If you hear noises in the middle of a wood, don't investigate them.
11. Don't check under the bed or in cupboards; get some other sucker to do it.
12. Never buy anything that has the first name *Magic* or *Gigantic*.
13. If your name is *Beauty* make it clear you hate roses, unless they've come from a shop.

14. Avoid women with green snaky hair. Only look at them in mirrors.
15. If anything with too many legs, arms, eyes or heads speaks to you, ignore it.
16. If anyone, apart from your parents, tells you they're gonna' eat you up, believe them.
17. If your parents have a distant look about them (Look up Zombies and Alien Possession), believe them too.
18. Don't hug anything hairy with rotten table manners, unless it's your dad.
19. Wrap yourself in cotton wool.
20. Wear deodorant, to stop them smelling your fear.

NOTE: NO RESPONSIBILITY WILL BE TAKEN
FOR ANYONE WHO IGNORES THIS NOTICE.

P.S. Always wear a coat over your cotton wool or you might attract the wrong kind of attention.
Thank you for listening.

Sue Hardy-Dawson

If You Dare to Dine with Dinosaurs:

Funny Poems About Dinosaurs & Dragons

The Spaghettisaur

Most dinosaurs look strange
Most dinosaurs look weird
But I'm afraid, this one looks worse
Than anybody feared
Long spindly legs like shoelaces
Thin tail drags on the floor
Has arms and hands like rubber bands
She's called Spaghettisaur
The longest, skinniest dinosaur
That you ever did see
She lived in the Noodle Desert
(Which later became Italy)
Other predators tried to eat her
She tasted delicious of course
As down her nose, she sometimes blows
A rich tomato sauce
All Spaghettisaurs died out long ago
Which was a huge disaster
We aren't too sure why, but don't fret or cry
As that's all in the pasta . . .

Chris White

Dear Mr and Mrs T. Rex,

It is with regret that I find it necessary
to write to you once AGAIN
about Tyronne's unsociable behaviour
in the School Dinner Hall.

This term alone he has devoured
nine classmates, four teachers, two dinner ladies
and possibly Mr MacIntosh, the janitor
who has not been seen since last Tuesday.

While it is lovely to see a growing boy with a healthy
    appetite,
I must ask you to have a word with him.
I am running out of supply teachers
and have had to deal with some rather annoyed parents.

Perhaps he could have a more substantial breakfast
or an extra snack for playtime.
I could provide you with some delicious vegetarian
    alternatives
which are both healthy and filling.

I would be very grateful if you could be so kind
as to reply to me by email on this matter
as I am still missing a leg
from the last meeting we had in my office.

Kindest regards and warmest wishes,
Benedict Brontosaurus (Dip D Ed)
Headmaster
Jurassic Academy

PS. Please do let me know if my leg ever makes a
    'reappearance.'
PPS. May I also take this opportunity to remind you that
    the school fete is a week on Saturday?
Your rock cakes went down a treat last year.

BB x

Julie Douglas

Dining with Dinosaurs

If you dare
to dine with dinosaurs
explain ● it's rude to
eat \/\/\/\/\/\/\/\/\/\/\/\
front
doors, /\/\/\/\/\/\/\/\/\/\/\
and if they make holes in
your floors, never
reward
them with applause.
Their tiny brains can hardly think,
so never let them play   with   ink,
and discourage paddling
in the sink or tipping toilets
up to drink. It's hard to stop
them chewing chairs and
damaging the hall and stairs,
importantly such small repairs,
should   never   catch
you unawares.   But if   you
dine   with   dinosaurs,
you   may find   that it's
good   to pause,   and
  before   you let
    them
      all
    indoors
  make
    sure
      that
        they
          are
            herbivores

Sue Hardy-Dawson

Dragon Air

Hello young man and welcome
To this flight with Dragon Air,
The fastest way to travel
And the best thing – there's no fare!

That's right; no money, gratis, free!
So climb upon my back.
Relax and thank your lucky stars . . .
My Little In-Flight Snack.

Matt Goodfellow

The Toaster

A silver-scaled dragon with jaws flaming red
Sits at my elbow and toasts my bread.
I hand him fat slices, and then, one by one,
He hands them back when he sees they are done.

William Jay Smith

The Dragon in the Cellar

There's a dragon!
There's a dragon!
There's a dragon in the cellar!
Yeah, we've got a cellar-dweller.
There's a dragon in the cellar.

He's a cleanliness fanatic,
Takes his trousers and his jacket
To the dragon from the attic
Who puts powder by the packet
In a pre-set automatic
With a rattle and a racket
That's disturbing and dramatic.

There's a dragon!
There's a dragon!
There's a dragon in the cellar!
With a flame that's red 'n' yeller,
There's a dragon in the cellar . . .

. . . and a dragon on the roof
Who's only partly waterproof,
So she's borrowed an umbrella
From the dragon in the cellar.

There's a dragon!
There's a dragon!
There's a dragon in the cellar!
If you smell a panatela
It's the dragon in the cellar.

And the dragon from the study's
Helping out his cellar buddy
Getting wet and soap-suddy,
With the dragon from the loo
There to give a hand too,
While the dragon from the porch
Supervises with a torch,
Though the dragon from the landing
Through a slight misunderstanding
Is busy paint-stripping and sanding.

There's a dragon!
There's a dragon!
There's a dragon in the cellar!
Find my dad and tell the feller
There's a dragon in the cellar . . .

. . . where the dragon from my room
Goes zoom, zoom, zoom
In a cloud of polish and spray perfume
Cos he's the dragon whom
They pay to brighten up the gloom
With a mop and a duster and a broom, broom, broom.

There's a dragon!
There's a dragon!
There's a dragon in the cellar!
Gonna get my mum and tell her
There's a dragon in the cellar.

Nick Toczek

Dinodictionary

A dinosaur that's really dull
Is called a Dinobore
On the front of their houses
You'll find a Dinodoor
They get their food and other goods
From the local Dinostore
If they argue and all fall out
They start a Dinowar
If one should fly up in the sky
It's called a Dinosoar
When playing football, the result
Is called the Dinoscore
The creamy mix of veg they eat?
Well, that's some Dinoslaw
Doing jobs around the house?
That's a Dinochore
If one trips up and hurts its knee
Then 'Ouch!' it's Dinosore
Or maybe have a cheeky nap
You'll hear a Dinosnore
If one roars out a naughty word
I'm afraid they Dinoswore
All this is true, I'm telling you
And that's the Dinolaw.

Chris White

The Dino Disco

From Zanzibar to San Francisco
all the Raptors twirl 'n twisto
to a stomp 'n romp calypso
dance floors crumble into bits-o!

Man, those Megadons can mambo,
boy, those Brontos truly tango
oh what fun when they fandango
strumming their Jurassic banjo!

Best of all, a beastly conga
claw-to-tail a mega monster
to a slinky, funky number
all that crashing sounds like thunder!

When those reptiles twirl and twist-o
how they heave their mighty hips-o
at the mighty ballroom blitz-o
come on down . . . the DINO DISCO!

James Carter

Dinosaurs Are Still Alive!

Dinosaurs are still alive!
It's true – It's NOT a dream!
You can see them every Saturday
In our local football team . . .

Trevor Harvey

A Ghost Went Out Haunting One Saturday Night:

Funny Spooky Poems

Hallowe'en

Darren's got a pumpkin
Hollowed out a treat
He put it in the window
It scared half the street

I wish I had a pumpkin
But I've not and it's a shame
I've got a scary carrot
But it's not the same

Roger Stevens

A Ghost Went Out Haunting

A ghost went out haunting one Saturday night,
a horrible grim, gloomy, green, ghastly sight.
It seeped into bedrooms, it sidled through walls
with howls, hoots and hollers, bellows and bawls.
But no one was frightened, they all acted bored.
The ghost was upset, hurt, offended, ignored
till a girl scoffed, 'Our movies are scarier than you.'
and chased it away with a sarcastic, 'Boo!'
It stared at its watch. It was only eleven
and in a great huff, took the first train to heaven.

Marian Swinger

The Relentless Pursuit of the 12-Toed Snortliblog

It SNIFFS you out: 'sfft, sfft, sfft'
It HEARS your heartbeat: 'dup dup dup'
It SEES your terror: 'aaaaaah!'
It TASTES revenge: 'mmmmmmmmmmmm'

It will grab you with all twelve toes . . .

It will give you a big kiss:
  'SHSPPLUKKLSSMLOOPSCHPPWASSSSHLAKKK'!

Anon

The Phantom Kiss

There's a phantom kiss on the loose,
you could find it in your house.
It flits about like a fly,
it scuttles about like a mouse.
It hides in gloomy corners
till someone turns out the light,
so you won't be able to see it
in the darkness of the night.
But the phantom kiss will be there
and you won't hear it speak your name,
but if it calls and it touches you,
you will never be the same!

Like a vampire that turns you into its own,
the phantom kiss will claim you.
Just a gentle brush of lips on your cheek
is all that it takes to inflame you.
You'll be wanting to kiss
everyone you see,
be it greatest friend
or deepest enemy.

If the phantom kiss
holds you in its power,
you won't shrug it off
in a minute or an hour.
It will hold you tight
in its embarrassing grip
while you kiss all around you
on cheek or on lips.

So remember if your mum's
always kissing you,
you'll realise now
that she was touched too.
And serial kissers
like your aunts and your gran
you'll realise this
was how they began.

And someone who may have been touched too
is the person sitting next to you . . .

Brian Moses

Sam Spook

(the curse of all teachers)

Sammy was a teacher-spook
And he spooked around in schools
Spooking out for teachers
In class
     At desks
          On stools . . .

He'd wriggle up their trouser legs
He'd make them jump and squeal
And turn them into funny things
Like mud
       Or orange peel.

He'd turn them into awful things
Cabbages and flies
Bits of string and paper
Bits of chewed-up pies!
Miss Thompson was a sausage
Miss Cummins was a clock
Miss Angel was a plughole
Miss Ryan was a sock!

He'd turn them into ANYTHING
     so be careful where you tread –
That custard could be teacher . . .
And that apple core –
        The Head!

Peter Dixon

Feeding Fred

I used to spend bedtimes in dread
A monster lived under my bed
Till one night last week
He started to speak.
And said, 'Nice to meet you, I'm Fred'

'I'm sorry I gave you a fright
'I'm just looking round for a bite
'Your room is so neat
'There's nothing to eat
'And I need a snack in the night'

So now I make sure I feed Fred
By hiding mess under my bed
As part of the deal
Fred gets a square meal
And frightens my sister instead

Mary Evans

The Ghoul Inspectre's Coming

The Ghoul
Inspectre's coming,
dust off ● ● your lazy
bones, tidy out your coffins,
polish up your mournful moans.
Practise ribcages rattles, check that your chains
'ill clank, gibber when you're spoken to and keep your cell ars dank.
Display your bat collection and cobweb-hanging
talents – freshen up the bloodstains, see
that the spook books balance.
Hover to attention, grease
your glides and brush
your mould – the
Ghoul Inspectre's
coming, make
sure his
welcome's
Cold!

Liz Brownlee

Advertisement from the Ghostly Gazette

There's a special place where you can stay
when your haunting is over each night,
it's a spooky spooktacular guest house
where you'll sleep away the light.

In each room the curtains are shut
so the sun's rays never slip through.
We guarantee you a good day's sleep
with nothing disturbing you.

There's a hook on the back of your door
where if you've lost your head
your eyes can still watch over you
while your body rests in bed.

We have rooms with very tall ceilings
for ghosts who levitate
and to make you feel among friends
we can colour co-ordinate,

Grey ladies stay in one room
and green ladies in another.
Poltergeists are soundproofed
so they only disturb each other.

For those who like walking through walls
and would rather not use the door
Please feel free to enter this way
or even rise up through the floor.

We can cater for every need
and we're sure that you'll love it here.
Just don't forget to pay the bill
before you disappear!

Brian Moses

Halloween Date from Hell

I'm sick of chopping creatures up.
I'm tired of making broth
filled with bleedin' legs of frog
and flaky wings of moth.

So I bought the *Undead Times* last week
and clawed the classifieds
go find a date for Halloween –
an ugly one who's died!

Being the busiest time of year
the list was not the most –
a mischief-seeking goblin,
a bored, retired ghost.

Confused and lonely werewolf types
who couldn't do full moons,
a vampire who'd prefer to not
do sunny afternoons.

A pumpkin-monster desperate
for airheads with a grin,
a skeleton who'd like to meet
a slim girl thin on skin.

I was just about to give up when . . .
right there on the next page
was a gorgeous, grotesque zombie
thirteen times my age.

My wrinkly heart began to beat.
His search was for a hag
with warts and boils and super-nose
who liked to dress in rags.

It couldn't be more perfect!
We met All Hallows Eve.
But when he kissed my veiny hand
his arm fell from his sleeve.

Silence first, but then we laughed.
It echoed in the doom.
He dragged me to the picnic
he'd laid out on his tomb.

We crunched on bats and vultures' beaks.
He boasted he's a killer
and that he was an extra once
In Michael Jackson's *Thriller*.

A love like this I'd never known.
He lurched me to my door.
He soaked me with a goodnight kiss.
His tongue fell on the floor.

The local kids fled from the streets
and gangs of adults too.
I beckoned in my juicy hunk
to taste my special brew.

He grunted to the kitchen stove.
The cauldron bubbled hot.
I stroked his chest, then shoved him hard
with all the strength I'd got.

Well, I'm sick of chopping creatures up,
I'm tired of making broth.
But zombies are much easier
As bits of them fall off.

No fiddly scraps of moth or frog,
no complicated spell,
just a gristly, grisly Halloween stew –
A match sure made in hell!

Mark Bird

164

You Pulled Me Out of a Black Hole:

Funny Poems About Space

Announcing the Guests at the Space Beasts' Party

'The Araspew from Bashergrannd'
'The Cakkaspoo from Danglebannd'
'The Eggisplosh from Ferrintole'
'The Gurglenosh from Hiccupole'
'The Inkiblag from Jupitickle'
'The Kellogclag from Lamandpickle'
'The Mighteemoose from Nosuchplace'
'The Orridjuice from Piggiface'
'The Quizziknutt from Radishratt'
'The Spattersplut from Trikkicatt'
'The Underpance from Verristrong'
'The Willidance from Xrayblong'
'The Yuckyspitt from Ziggersplitt'

Wes Magee

Aliens Stole My Underpants

To understand the ways
of alien beings is hard,
and I've never worked it out
why they landed in my backyard.

And I've always wondered why
on their journey from the stars,
these aliens stole my underpants
and took them back to Mars.

They came on a Monday night
when the weekend wash had been done,
pegged out on the line
to be dried by the morning sun.

Mrs Driver from next door
was a witness at the scene
when aliens snatched my underpants –
I'm glad that they were clean!

It seems they were quite choosy
as nothing else was taken.
Do aliens wear underpants
or were they just mistaken?

I think I have a theory
as to what they wanted them for,
they needed to block off a draught
blowing in through the spacecraft door.

Or maybe some Mars museum
wanted items bought back from space.
Just think, my pair of Y-fronts displayed
in their own glass case.

And on the label beneath
would be written where they got 'em
and how such funny underwear
once covered an Earthling's bottom!

Brian Moses

Shed in Space

My Grandad Lewis
On my mother's side
Had two ambitions.
One was to take first prize
For shallots at the village show
And the second
Was to be a space commander.
Every Tuesday
After I'd got their messages,
He'd lead me with a wink
To his garden shed
And there, amongst the linseed
And the sacks of peat and horse manure
He'd light his pipe
And settle in his deck chair.
His old eyes on the blue and distant
That no one else could see,
He'd ask,
'Are we A-OK for lift-off?'
Gripping the handles of the lawnmower
I'd reply:
'A-OK.'
And then facing the workbench,
In front of shelves of paint and creosote
And racks of glistening chisels
He'd talk to Mission Control.
'Five-Four-Three-Two-One-Zero –

We have lift-off.
This is Grandad Lewis talking,
Do you read me?
Britain's first space shed
Is rising majestically into orbit
From its launch pad
In the allotments
Of Lakey Lane.'

And so we'd fly
Through timeless afternoons
Till teatime came
Amongst the planets
And mysterious suns,
While the world
Receded like a dream:
Grandad never won
That prize for shallots,
But as the captain
Of an intergalactic shed
There was no one to touch him.

Gareth Owen

The Astronaut Near Me

There's an astronaut who lives near me –
I wonder how he's feeling.
I see him walk, from time to time,
upon his front room ceiling.

There's an astronaut who lives near me –
he's always seemed quite fair,
but I've watched him wear a goldfish bowl
and dry shampoo his hair.

There's an astronaut who lives near me –
a postman often knocks
and, when the door is opened up,
delivers piles of rocks.

There's an astronaut who lives near me –
his house is quite the tip,
as though he flew here in the dark
and had to crash his ship.

There's an astronaut who lives near me –
he drives the fastest cars,
he sometimes waves and I wave back
as I'm blasting off to Mars!

Dom Conlon

My Granddad Burt's an Alien

My granddad Burt's an alien,
he came from outer space
with a dodgy hip in a rocket ship
to save the human race

His skin's as green as a green string bean
with shades of mushy pea
and his beard is grey,
as is the way for an OAP ET

His arms protrude like Super Noodles,
long and thin and wobbly
I hesitate to state which flavour
(ham and mushroom prob'ly)

He wears a cap and a jetpack mac
with boots and baggy kecks
and says he gets his X-ray specs
from Boots on Planet X

He's highly wise, advising guys
on how to help mankind
He's more astute than Doctors Who,
Where, When and Why combined

He knocks the socks off Brian Cox,
makes Mister Spock look tame
You'll never find a finer mind
behind a Zimmer frame

Some days he beams me up from school
aboard his flying saucer,
my mates all say it's way more cool
than mummy's Vauxhall Corsa

And so at three we go for tea
in zero gravity,
he seems to be the first ET
to eat a Maccy D

All the staff take photographs
of granddad's UFO
when in the queue for a drive-through brew
and Happy Meal to go

We scoff our fries and off we fly
at twice the speed of light
He takes a right at a satellite
then tucks me in at night

He tells me tales of comet trails
and stories from the stars
of robot chums with laser guns
(set to stun) on Mars

Then once he spies I've closed my eyes
he knows the day is done
and sets off home to get curtains drawn
at Area 51

He doesn't care to take the stair lift
when he goes to bed,
his rocket slippers get him quicker
up the stairs instead

He counts his sheep in hyper sleep
then gets up REALLY early
My granddad Burt's an alien . . .
and so's my grandma Shirley

Dale Neal

little Green Men

I just don't know what to do
about all these little green men,
they follow me into town and then
they follow me home again.
I find them queuing at the bus stop
or waiting to catch a train,
these groups of little green men,
all of them looking the same.

They queue with me in the post office
buying stamps for strange-sounding places,
their green little grins fixed permanently
upon their green little faces

I think these little green men
must be on a special mission,
but I just can't shake them off
I'm too far out of condition.
They run with me when I run,
always keeping me in sight.
They glow really bright in the dark
so I can't escape them at night.

My stress levels and my patience
are really being tested
I ought to phone the police
and have them all arrested.

But it makes no difference at all
if I rave or if I rant,
once little green men stole
my underpants,

now it looks like they're back
for me.

Brian Moses

The Alien Wedding

When the aliens got married,
The bride was dressed in zeet;
And with a flumzel in her groyt,
She really looked a treat.

The groom was onngy spoodle,
He felt a little quenz;
The best man told him not to cronk
In front of all their friends.

The bride's ensloshid father
Had slipped down too much glorter;
He grobbled up the aisle alone,
Then flomped back for his daughter.

The lushen bridesmaids followed
With such wigantic walks;
Their optikacious oggers
Were sparkling on their stalks.

The bride and groom entroathed their splice,
They swapped a little squip;
Then he splodged her on the kisser,
And she flimped him on the blip.

And after the wedding breakfast,
The stroadling and the laughter,
The loving pair took off to Mars
And splayed winkerly ever after.

Mike Jubb

An Alien Limerick

As on Red Planet, Mars, we alighted,
   A very large banner we sighted.
      'That's the answer,' I said.
      ' To why Mars is called "red".'
It said MARTIANS ALL LOVE MAN UNITED.

Eric Finney

The Blob

And . . . what is it like?

   Oh, it's scary and fatbumped
   And spike-eared and groany.
   It's hairy and face-splumped
   And bolshy and bony.

And . . . where does it live?

   Oh, in comets and spaceships
   And pulsars and black holes
   In craters and sheepdips
   And caverns and north poles.

And . . . what does it eat?

   Oh, roast rocks and fishlegs
   And X-rays and mooncrust.
   Then steel meat and sun-eggs
   And lava and spacedust.

And . . . who are its enemies?

   Oh, Zonkers and Moonquakes
   And Sunquarks and Zigbags.
   Dumb duncers and Milkshakes
   And Smogsters and Wigwags.

And . . . and . . . what does it wear?

Not a thing!
It's bare!

Wes Magee

Acknowledgements

The compiler and publisher would like to thank the following for permission to use copyright material:

'The Astronaut Near Me' by Don Conlon first published in *This Rock, That Rock* (Troika 2020); 'Twenty Ways to Avoid Monsters and Mythical Beasts' and 'Dining with Dinosaurs' by Sue Hardy-Dawson first published in *Where Zebras Go* by (Otter-Barry Books 2017); 'Three Bears Vs Goldilocks' by Laura Much first published in *Dear Ugly Sisters* (Otter-Barry Books 2020);'The Invisible Man's Invisible Dog' from *Thawing Frozen Frogs* by Brian Patten. Copyright ©Brian Patten. Reproduced by permission of the author c/o Rogers, Coleridge & White Ltd., 20 Powis Mews, London W11 1JN; 'The Car Trip' by Michael Rosen from *The Hypnotiser* (©Michael Rosen 1988) is printed by permission of United Agents (www.unitedagents.co.uk) on behalf of Michael Rosen; 'I Don't Like Poetry' by Joshua Siegal first published in *I Don't Like Poetry* by Bloomsbury; 'Hamster Man' by Kate Wakeling first published in *Moon Juice* (The Emma Press)

Every effort has been made to trace the copyright holders, but if any have been inadvertently overlooked the publisher will be pleased to make the necessary arrangement at the first opportunity.

About the Author

Brian Moses has been labelled 'one of Britain's favourite children's poets' by the National Poetry Archive. He has worked as a professional poet since 1988, performing his poetry and percussion shows in schools, libraries, theatres and festivals around the UK and abroad. He was asked by CBBC to write a poem for the Queen's 80th Birthday, invited by Prince Charles to speak at the Prince's Summer conference at Cambridge University and is founder and co-director of a national able writers' scheme in schools. He has written or edited over 200 books including *Lost Magic: The Very Best of Brian Moses* (Macmillan)